THE LIFE AND TIMES OF A
BLACK GARAGE DOOR GUY

THE LIFE AND TIMES OF A
BLACK GARAGE DOOR GUY

V LEIGH

To order additional copies of this book, contact:
Xlibris
844-714-8691
www.Xlibris.com
Orders@Xlibris.com
819561

CONTENTS

Acknowledgments.. xi

Chapter 1   Humm, Let Me Ponder A Profession......................... 1
Chapter 2   Chomped.. 7
Chapter 3   A Horse with No Name 13
Chapter 4   The Beckoning 15
Chapter 5   Mormon Sirens 19
Chapter 6   "No Niggers Allowed!" 23
Chapter 7   Witwe... 25
Chapter 8   Now I See.. 29
Chapter 9   "Yo', Daddy!" 31
Chapter 10   Dry Wall 37
Chapter 11   When You Do For The Least Of These 41
             Part 1.   Fallen between the Cracks................................ 41
             Part 2.   Elder Neglect 43
             Part 3.   House Arrest.. 45
             Part 4.   Homeless in the Hood 46
             Part 5.   Midwest Sistah.. 50
             Part 6.   Homeless in "Mexicali" 53
             Part 7.   Homeless in A Car 55
             Part 8.   The Last of the Good Samaritan..................... 56

Chapter 12   Creepiest Customers.. 59
             Part 1.   S&M Success 59
             Part 2.   The Fetish 60

Chapter 13   360 63

Chapter 14   "Oh Lordy" 67

Chapter 15   Close Encounters 73

Chapter 16   Cloverleaf Intersection 79

Chapter 17   Grim Reaper 83

Chapter 18   "Dad Said" 85

Chapter 19   Sole Brotha 89

Chapter 20   I Believe in Miracles...................................... 91

*Let the Lord be magnified which hath pleasure in the
prosperity of His servant. Psalm 35:27 KJV*

In loving memory of my uncle James Peter Williams.
RIP, dear Po' Pete.

ACKNOWLEDGMENTS

It would truly be remiss of me, dear Lord God, to *not* give You all the honor, glory, and praise for granting me this first-in-a-lifetime writing success.

Thank you, my sweet Jesus!

I am eternally grateful to my precious mother, Erma Lee (Tuta), who crossed over Jordan way too soon at the tender age of twenty-six; to my dearest, sweetest ever, steadfast Grandma Alberta, my rock; to my dependable ole Unka Pete and his amazing wife, my dearest caring Auntie C.

I sincerely appreciate all my dad intended for my good and thank my nurturing stepmom, Sweet Lorraine, my sole port in the storm, for all she did on my behalf throughout my life, especially the invaluable Morgan Park Holy Name of Mary Parochial School education she provided me.

I thank everyone of you for pouring your very best into me. I can only trust that each of you look down upon me with humbled pride.

Thank you, my darling "Honey", for your genuine love and faith in my God-given gifts which enabled me to reach this epic milestone. Words cannot evoke the deep feelings I have exclusively for you, my husband of over forty years, my handsome, Black knight in shining armor, the one true love of my life, Rufus, Sr. My love for you is the definitive definition of "unconditional." No one could ever, possibly love you more than I do. Know that I deeply respect you and all you do for me. No one could ask for a more dedicated spouse than you have proven to be to me, especially financially. I constantly thank God for our "three-fold cord", holy, union. God the Father, Rufus the husband/provider and "V" the devoted, loving wife.

I acknowledge "Mommy's" two forever cherished infants: my baby girl Tiyon and baby boy Maurice; both now in heaven's eternal rest, while always being carried deep within the two unfillable holes in my heart.

With love, motherly gratitude, and pride, I thank each of my devoted three surviving children: Lanair Sr., Deneè, and Adonis Sr. and his loving wife, our Detroit daughter-in-love, Nicola. Even though you'd never bring it up, your support of us both, whenever given, was always appreciated beyond measure.

God bless and keep my darling, sweet lil' sistah Deb. You and I grew up together in a home filled with love and Godly direction. "7 & 11"—that was us. You are my prayer warrior, and I am so blessed to have you in my life. We're loving sisters and indeed best friends. "Smooches".

My heartfelt thanks, to dear lil sis LPN Sharon (my "L"), for the gracious rides around town when I'd visit, and I'll never forget my custom corn rows—sheer perfection. You are a great auntie as well. I am grateful for *all* you did keeping your firstborn niece that week during that long, hot summer. "May the good Lord cause His face to shine down upon you," Psalms 4:6 KJV, all the days of your life. Love ya much, your very own Big Sis.

Thank you D, L's fraternal twin, for sharing endearing moments with my eldest, your nephew. May God bless you... with the love of CHRIST... Ephesians 3:19 KJV yvolBS

To you my captivating, firstborn, granddaughter my "Chatter" know that your GRNE V loves you immensely and prays for you regularly. XOXOs, sweetie pie. I am so proud of you and your many accomplishments. God be forever with you. My lovely, thoughtful gift, the tree painting is matted and framed on the kitchen wall.

God bless you dear firstborn grand, illustrious, military officer "Lennie" and wife, industrious teacher Rochelle and your spectacular 3 kids, genius Grandson Kendall and remarkable family, and my creative grand baby girl, "Chef J"; greater things await you so persevere. May each of you attain what God has for you, His (best) destiny. Phenomenal Lil' Don and fabulous Kyris pray daily for God to help you do His will, then do your very best. Trust me, He hears you. Practice living the two most important commandments written in red: "Love God with all your heart, soul, and mind, and love others as you do yourself." Matthew 22:35-40 KJV Love always, your very own GRNE V.

I respectfully salute my two deceased, favorite in-laws of all time: loyal Lola/Nana and delightful dear Cuz'n Ruth. RIP, 'til we meet again.

Thanks again and again, unforgettable A. LaToya, for your every kindness.

"Yay!" to my "true friends", ever-encouraging drum majors everyone: BSN Virginia, RN Judy, RN Elaine, Ms. Positivity and alumna "Ms." Georgia-Girrrlll (Go, 'Velt 66!), my FOMPI Coordinator Toy Ann, WPW, ICFC's Auntie Lettie, FUMC's Sister Margaret Clark, and Ms. Ruth in ole Sweet Home, AR. I praise God for you all!

Last but not least, thank you, Xlibris Publishing, for having the prudence to guide me to this point in my writing career.

May God bless you always, Consultant Sid Wilson.

CHAPTER 1

Humm, Let Me Ponder A Profession

This is my life. I was born in Chicago's Cook County General Hospital, but raised in Detroit. I grew up a bright eyed, bushy-tailed youngster filled with awe on the west of town. Our family moved to the less expensive east side when I was around seven. I was a dependable, neighborhood paperboy through high school. I then did two stints in the US Army. Even though I realized I did not have the temperament to pursue college, I still desired to make an honest living.

I'd managed to somehow beat the odds by living longer than many childhood associates who craved the fast life: Iroc Z's, sharp clothes, natty shoes, lots of money, and lots of fine chicks. I'd heard of far too many drug-gang-related shooting deaths, even decapitations, not to mention death-ending experiences involving the P-O-lice. Is it no wonder Black guys even make it all the way to high school commencement?

Sorry to say, post-90s, Black girls began trying to do jail time, with so many missing-in-action daddies in their homes, once the neighborhood Chrysler plant shut down and relocated in Pole town. A neighborhood chick would be either earmarked to be a homebody, most likely wed to a settled older dude, like back in the 50's, or go the coed route, determined to do better than your average high school student with a diploma, (hard enough to do in the hood), or opting out, like those guys who dropped out for whatever reason, later getting a GED. A few of the focused chicks did go on to become some type of professional: usually a teacher, nurse, legal system employee, office worker, even one media personality. Depending upon availability, one of the factories would hire a female. Back then, there would always be one or two teen moms on the block, forever searching for that perfect man to be a dad to all the other men's kids she had along the way. Many of them at least would feed their kids, and not sell the monthly food stamps. You'd hear it through the grape vine, they had fewer, if any abortions. Everybody knew the 'chicken head's' business. These were beat down young females who felt trapped; and traded their precious bodies more so for drugs. They felt their young, Black lives didn't matter, tragic. There was no telling what was going on behind their closed doors. Taking hard drugs seemed to for the moment, ease the pain, I guess. Another reason sometimes more chicks died than dudes was due to the horrible death rate among Black moms of all ages and their newborns, if not stillborns. Anyway, to paraphrase Malcom, basically, Black females are seen as the bottom of the food chain. The ghetto girls sometimes ended up far worse off than the guys, if they lived long enough to grow up.

As for me, there was no way you'd ever find me up on any corner slinging anything. Still wet behind the ears, I found it exciting to serve in Alaska, in artillery. Twenty/twenty hindsight says I should have not listened to my recruiter and instead went into cooking. That would have provided me greater opportunity in the real world than gunnery ever could. Lots of the other guys in the hood teased me when they found out I was going into "Uncle Sam's Army". When I left, they were up on the co'na'; when I returned from basic, if alive, they were still up on the co'na'.

My patience had run out wishing for mega bucks to fall in my lap, for a shiny car, while hoping for the chance to date really hot chicks, with curvy bodies and shapely big butts. I know big girls need love too, but I had made more than my share of donations over the years to that charity just to get by. I looked forward to seeing the guys on the block when I came home after basic at Fort Sill in my fine fur coats with matching fur hats, looking like a new breed Youngblood in Superfly. I'd become a marksman and a terrific knife fighter as well, but that's a whole 'notha' book unto itself.

I then did a unremarkable tour of duty in California before reentering the real world. Once my time in the military was up, there was still no direction or sense of purpose for me. As I continued aging, I found myself floating from one meaningless office job to the next, experiencing failed marriages and producing two great kids along the way. After almost a year of bad luck in New York, my lil' sister sent me a one-way plane ticket to Phoenix, Arizona, her new hometown. She was busy working on her B.B.A. Later she obtained her M.B.A. before becoming a rising star, Peace Officer in the Harris County Sheriff's Department, Houston, Texas. Twelve years after relocating from Arizona, I finally convinced her to join me in Houston, Texas until she could find a promising job since ole California no longer offered her endless opportunities even with her M.B.A.

Thanks Sis!

By the way, our younger brother is a skilled cement finisher, who has his CDL, and runs a construction crew in Michigan.

Hey Bro.

Now back to me, setting all that bouncing around aside, I finally decided to have a serious conversation with the man in the mirror. I asked myself hard questions and gave me honest answers.

"Well, you're not getting any younger. You're batting The hell outta your twenties, now what? Just exactly what type career do you think would be best for you? Maybe a trade? You know you're not college material. Speak up! I CAN'T HEAR YOU!"

Chuckles.

"Count your lucky stars, you've been offered the chance to train under a brotha who owns his own company. You'll never know if you don't at least give it your best shot! Go on. GO FOR IT!"

And so I did. It has been my personal work experience that Black men, people of color, overall, are not treated like equals in the workplace or anywhere else in America, let alone like human beings especially in New York City and Phoenix, AZ. Later I found Texas, of all places, to be the unexpected exception, where men are treated individually, instead of monolithically.

Way too many White men feel entitled to speak to brothas as if they are stupid or a big entertaining "coon," without integrity, hilariously laughing at their often attempts to tell a sense-of-entitlement or sordid, hillbilly joke, taking their many insults in stride, but why should we? It is so obvious to me that if you are a visibly Black man, then according to "the powers that be," you don't deserve an honest job, let alone a trade; you deserve to be hardly making it, if at all. You ought to be living hand to mouth, harassed at someone else's whim, only to be criticized for not taking care of your responsibilities, while at the same time, scuffling for a crust of bread to feed yourself, let alone a wife and family; that's if you weren't particular about procreating the species in or outside of the sanctioning church. I've never been one to conform to the masses simply because, if anything

I'd look for some way to distinguish myself from the pack. No, I didn't mind being labeled different, or difficult if the situation called for it. I've never been a status quo guy.

To quote a wise wordsmith of our time, I must totally agree with Cube: "My skin is my sin."

After completing the basics, I began training under a regional company's experienced techs, all White. I felt I had made another big mistake until I was paired with this one Hispanic guy.

At first, it was a clash of the titans, but somewhere along the way, we buried the hatchet, and I was able to swallow my pride and learn from that hotheaded El Salvadorian Erick. The name fit him perfectly.

He told me it meant "complete ruler." I appreciate all he taught me and made a point of telling him so. I worked a few years at companies before branching out on my own for a while. One thing I know for sure: How great it is to go solo. Sure it's more responsibility with no assistant, but more importantly, mo' money in my pocket.

Some may ask, "What made you think you, a Black man, should get a job installing garage doors, especially with White companies, servicing mostly White, non-Black customers?"

My response: 3 little words-"money-solo-honesty".

CHAPTER 2

Chomped

I'd had quite a weekend and not in a good sense. I was a few seconds late, feeding my meter, and a Hispanic-looking tow truck driver had already began to hook my commercial van to tow it. I rushed over to stop him, but he'd already began lifting it. So, we ended up in a physical scuffle. Unable to reason with him, to not take away my livelihood, I punched him, and the police were called.

A big, Black cop with a limp answered the call and arrested me for assault. He read me my rights and informed me of the law broken, then yanked me up from behind to handcuff me real rough.

I immediately told him, "Look, I'm *not* resisting!"

He then slacked off with the overzealousness. I was released on my own recognizance, and sentenced to community service for 6 weeks, during which time I felt I made a difference in the neighborhood, patching and painting bus stop benches and shelters around the parish.

That unpleasant incident took me back to two awful times I tangled with the Detroit P-O-lice when I was 8 and 9 years old. One day as I waited for the light to turn green at the corner, next to of all places, the 9th precinct, a marked police car hugged the curb as it turned past me, and the White uniformed cop driving, harked up and spit in my face as he howled flooring the car down the street. His partner was chuckling like a clown.

When I was nine, coming home from Sunday School and church, a unmarked Chevy Caprice slowed to a stop across the street from me, and the fat, White plains clothed detective behind the wheel grinned and told me in a harsh tone to come over, he wanted to tell me something important. I was of course hesitant, but he flashed his badge. As soon as I reached his window, he snatched my long tie and slowly accelerated on down the street, dragging me along. The only thing which saved me from further humiliation, and harm was the group of folks standing around down the block just hanging out. The cop's partner smiled along; but did not look too thrilled. Suddenly my tie was released causing me to tumble and stumble and fall down in the street, scuffing my Sunday best shoes and tearing big holes in my dress pants, scarring up my knees and hands and chin. It was still early and luckily no traffic was coming either way. Were my folks ever irate both times, but with no details there was nothing to be done when they tried to file a report. For the longest I feared the police whenever I was out alone, walking or on my bike.

Sometime later, I recognized running into that same cop years before when I worked at the "Big House" prison in Florence, AZ as a Corrections Officer. Back then, he was stationed at the entry gate; only he didn't have a limp at the time. That would have been a ideal gig for me to work my way up similar to my sister, but I just couldn't take the crooked politics, and without a degree, it would have taken me forever to be promoted a second time. It would have been like me trying to run for US president, a big mess!

I may have thought my weekend was as bad as it gets, but little did I know what awaited me on my job that Monday. That Monday my job had prescheduled my first appointment, notifying the homeowners a day in advance. I called on the day of install, but they said they were out and about but assured me they would be home in a half hour.

I was instructed to enter by the side door into the garage to set up. I had my reservations, but surprisingly, my Caucasian boss unwisely flip-flopped and agreed with the Caucasian couple's instructions on the three-way call.

Reluctantly, I entered against my "queasy belly" inkling. The garage repair trapped me inside the building, besides a slim side door in and out.

As soon as I set foot on the property, I could clearly hear deep, loud barking resonating from inside the house. As I set up my tools, I noticed a huge "doggy door" over by the washer and dryer. I thought; "That door looks big enough for a grown leopard or jaguar to crash through." The door had no bottom. I assumed it had to be locked from the inside.

Back then, I was a young, wiry newbie. Suddenly, a giant black and brown Bullmastiff busted through the huge doggy door and voraciously attacked me, latching on to my left ankle and foot. He tossed me back and forth like a rag doll before flinging me across the room.

Understand I am a true dog lover, but out of sheer desperation, I had no other choice than to protect myself. After landing on my tool bag, I pulled out my claw hammer and began wailing on his midsection, undoubtably doing internal damage, but that didn't slow him down one bit. As soon as I saw I was able to finally reach his head, I had the presence of mind to pull out my razor-sharp box cutter and sliced his face from the tip of one eye down across his nose, slicing his nose clean off.

He immediately released me from his vice grip and ran yelping back through the same way he'd entered. The garage was a virtual blood bath.

I was left dazed, probably in shock. My injuries were severe. I used a old tee shirt to tourniquet my injuries, then hobbled my way around, gathering up my things.

Upon my second and final trip to the garage, about two minutes after being attacked, guess who finally arrived? The husband joined me inside of the garage, seeking details. He was genuinely concerned at first, until his wife came running out of the house hysterical, riling him up to kill me!

I got out of there as fast as possible and called my boss to explain while driving myself straight to the AZ VA, where they x-rayed me, cleaned and stitched up my gapping wounds, bandaged me up good, and gave me a barrage of shots. They offered me a pair of crutches, which I declined because I needed to continue working, a quad cane had to do me.

My boss was sympathetic at first, telling me to bring in my doctor's report. He admitted he recalled them giving me instructions to enter their side door before they made it home.

He told me they called the police but lied, denying any such consent for me to pre-enter. He also gave my home address to a detective who followed up with me at my place.

I gave my detailed account of the unfortunate incident. Initially, my boss told the police the truth about the couple telling me to enter before they made it home.

Then about six months later, the boss reneged on his original, true version after being sued. Regrettably, they had to have their beloved Attila put down.

There was a court hearing; although I was never summoned, but rather unceremoniously "let go." I remain sorry over having to mortally wound one of "man's best friends" who was simply doing his job, but you "true blue animal lovers" tell me, what else could anybody have done? Unchallenged, he would have most certainly mauled me to death.

CHAPTER 3

A Horse with No Name

A AZ company I briefly worked for often prescheduled me to go out for door installs with owners of rental property; such was the case when I was sent out to install some garage replacement doors for a barn. It was the owner's responsibility to pass on the pertinent info to all parties residing on the premises. This was pre-cell phone days. Protocol dictated I keep the appointment, even if I got no answer when I tried calling ahead from the warehouse, to announce my ETA; logic being the occupant-tenant could be on the premises, perhaps in an outbuilding.

Such was the case regarding this particular assignment. When I arrived, there was no answer to the doorbell. Having been assured someone would be home, I then drove my commercial van around the dusty road toward the back where I saw a big red barn. I got out and walked toward the slightly ajar barn doors and slowly ventured in.

There were a few stalls with various types of horses in them. I called out to introduce myself as I strolled through, but I soon came across a stall with a middle-aged rather frumpy-looking White woman, somehow positioned on a few bales of hay, legs spread wide open. Standing above her was a full-grown, erect, beautiful black stallion. The woman had both hands firmly gripped around a very, large, throbbing, stiff-looking horse's penis.

As she rhythmically motioned up and down, I could swear that horse had the biggest smile on his face. Needless to say, I was outdone! Who would ever imagine discovering such an unnerving act. With a loss for words, I just said, "Oh sorry!'

Totally mortified, she turned beet red. She repeated the utterance: "No, I'm so sorry! I wasn't expecting anyone so soon."

I thought to myself, "No doubt."

She evidently was so wrapped up in the moment, she didn't have enough time to react to the sound of my voice. Knowing no doors would be installed there after all of that, I jumped in my truck and hightailed it on out of there. Of course, I'd heard of bestiality before. I'd even seen photos of such unnatural acts of women with big dogs, like a Great Dane and the like, but couldn't have ever imagined seeing a human actually hooked up with a dark coated, Mr. Ed.

I'd always thought horses were for riding, not pleasuring. The pressing issue at hand was how was I going to rationally explain why I did not do the job I was sent to do.

CHAPTER 4

The Beckoning

After I relocated to Houston, I was sent out on a nighttime emergency call to a ritzy gated community, full of estate homes. After making my routine office check-in call, I rang the fancy front doorbell.

A White guy who looked to be in his late twenties answered the door. I saw where he must have been camping out on the L-shaped, soft leather sofa in the living room, which to me, looked like a grand ballroom.

He had an odd look with an aura to match. I can't explain it, I wouldn't say he looked like a Down's Syndrome patient exactly, but there was a different vibe about him.

After introducing myself, I asked was he home alone, as to prevent any unexpected surprises. He said yes and proceeded to explain that a relative had driven his dad out of town to a family holiday gathering.

He told me to follow him through the kitchen to get to the garage entrance from inside the house. It was late December, and there were bright Christmas lights twinkling inside and outside of the house.

I followed him through a huge ornate formal dining room, into a sprawling 1990s kitchen on the other side of an old-fashioned swinging door. For some reason, Mammie in *Gone with the Wind* came to mind.

He then pointed towards the side door. There was a used Pathfinder parked to the side of a four- door garage. I drove my commercial van around through the auto-opened tall, wrought iron double gates.

Once inside the uber-organized garage, I admired an eye-poppin' jet black hot-off-the-line, Bentley Continental GT. I could picture myself stylin' behind the wheel, not driving Miss Daisy.

A year-old pure white Caddy CTS was parked next to the big dog. Once I was done with the repair, I rang the side doorbell, which had a different tone than the grand-sounding front one.

I found it odd there were no dogs around. Maybe they had hidden cameras for security.

My mind wandered for a second back to this older rich White lady's house, where in addition to cameras everywhere, she also had trained Dobermans at certain points inside and outside of her grand mansion. She lived alone by choice. She told me one gesture or word from her and they would devour the target without hesitation.

She didn't have to worry about me. I meant her no harm.

The same guy reappeared and buzzed me back in. I told him I was done and needed the payment info.

We ended up back in the ballroom, where he dialed his dad, said a few words, and handed me his cell. An older-sounding business type White guy gave me his credit card data. I thanked him and told him I would leave the receipt with his son.

He said, "Thank you," and hung up. I wasn't offered a seat, so I sat on the bottom two steps of the nearby grand spiral staircase, which looked like a big black hole up at the very top.

I'd forgotten to bring in my clipboard, so I asked for a book on which I could write the receipt, instead of on top of my hand. The guy quickly handed me one and disappeared for a second or two.

For some reason, the hairs on the back of my neck stood up, and I felt as if someone was staring down at me from the above abyss. I then glanced over my left shoulder, only to see a light green mist of some sort.

"What the . . . ?"

I completed the receipt as I called in the payment data, then left it on the stairs because as I followed the green stream from above, I saw floating down the staircase, the see-through spitting image of Linda Blair (a.k.a. Regan MacNiel) in full spooky, vivid green, split pea soup makeup as in *The Exorcist*. She was even wearing that same night gown. Without saying one single word, she held out both arms and beckoned with her hands for me to "Come to me."

Even more strange, the eerie music playing in the background was from Hitchcock's *Psycho* shower-slashing scene. "Eek, eek, eek!" I admit it, I screamed out loud, only not like a girl. I jumped straight up and shocked myself by sprinting faster than I had ever ran in my whole life!

Who knew I could pick 'em up and lay 'em down that fast in my forties? As I flew right past my host, I caught him actually slapping his thigh with one hand, cracking up on the sofa, laughing loudly, pointing at me with the other one.

I found my way back through the kitchen and soon arrived at my truck and burned rubber! I couldn't, for the life of me, figure out what the heck had just happened. I could hear The Twilight Zone playing in my head while zooming down the driveway!

Naturally, I never shared that with my job or anyone else for years. Many years later someone told me I had experienced a "hologram."

CHAPTER 5

Mormon Sirens

It was another blazing Mesa, AZ. day, beneath the searing sun's 110-degree temperature. My first assignment was a double door install in a middle-class Mormon neighborhood. I could tell it was going to be a slow day.

I always took my cooler full of bottled and canned non-alcoholic drinks of choice, plus a big jug with spout of iced H_2O, but depending upon the type of customer, I often opted to take them up on their hospitality. This would provide me with temporary AC, away from my packed truck.

Much to my surprise, not one, but two thinly-shaped young, blue-eyed, blondes welcomed me in for payment, after I finished the repair. They were first cousins, who almost looked like twins to me. They both looked younger than they were, like older teens.

The two brothers' daughters shared a well-kept duplex belonging to the older one's dad. Her age was twenty-two, and the other one was twenty-one. Tammie and Terri were their names. They both attended ASU in Phoenix but were out on summer break. Both worked part time in the family business, in local office supply stores. They let it be known neither wanted to get married anytime soon.

Each wore color-coordinated tennis outfits. Tammie's was pink and white with a short, pleated skirt. Terri was in a baby blue similar outfit. They said they were dressed to go to practice indoors later that afternoon. Each had her long locks pulled back in a high ponytail, with matching, tiny pearl earrings.

The living room was all done up in pink. They offered me a seat in a Jetson's type, chair as they both faced me from the couch.

When asked if I would like a cool drink, and what was my preference, my pat answer was always, "If you have anything nondiabetic, that would be great, thanks."

While Terri went to the nearby kitchen, Tammie handed me her Visa. I called it in and wrote out the receipt and handed it to her. They seemed interested in how I came to do garage doors, but they could have been just flirting.

I told them I just sort of fell into it, but I did like it as an honest living I could do solo, without having to pay a helper. Both women seemed surprised I was able to handle the "big doors" all by myself.

Lightly flexing my big guns, I shared with them an awe-shucks explanation: "As long as they are residential and not special-order commercial, no problem." They seemed or pretended to be fascinated.

While I gulped down my bottled sweet tea, I noticed right away the ever-so-innocent flinging of platinum hair and batting lashes. I tried playing it all off.

Once I was done with my drink, Tammie motioned for me to set the empty bottle on the end table, which I did. Then they both stood up and switched themselves on over toward an adjoining room, which looked like some sort of den or office, and asked me, in Double Mint twin voices, "Would you like to join us in the other room?"

To which, I, of course, replied, as any other red-blooded American male would, "Yes, lead the way. I'm right behind you."

Now mind you this was back in the heyday of my unfettered youth, in my fearless, foolish, early thirties. A straight back chair was already placed in the middle of the room, just waiting on me.

Top 100 Billboard tunes played softly in the background. The blinds were drawn.

There was a mid-watt bulb in a desk lamp already on. I couldn't stop my mind from racing. Maybe they had a Mandingo fantasy!

I'm not ashamed to say there stood one erect soldier at attention in the room. A sly grin plastered across my face as images of this being the beginning of some real freaky-deaky stuff tipped through my brain.

I peeped over my shoulder, searching for a closet, in case a hidden assassin lurked out of sight, but there was none. The thought of a hidden camera never even crossed my mind.

Unable to hold out much longer, imagine my disappointment as Terri went over to a bookcase and picked up what I thought was a King James and brought it over to me and began reading what sounded like scripture. She then passed it to her cousin, and Tammie took her turn doing the same.

They went back and forth at it, until I had to throw up both hands. "Okay, okay, ya got me. I give. I can't take no more!"

I dared to stand. Boy, if those two didn't have a big laugh at my expense.

Frankly, I had to smile at my own self. All my good Baptist Sunday school teaching must have flew the coop because what I thought was a Bible had to have been the Book of Mormon.

CHAPTER 6

"No Niggers Allowed!"

While working in Houston, I was sent to install a basic door for this particular, White couple. As soon as I met the little elderly wife, around eighty, I detected she was nervous but not because of me.

She kept rushing me, asking could I please try to finish up fast. I asked her, wasn't it more important that I do a good job?

She reluctantly agreed but kept looking back at the house. Almost as soon as I began setting up, a old cigar-smoking White man, for sure her husband, in his late eighties, burst through the backscreen door.

He was pushing a walker. She hurriedly excused herself and tried heading him off at the pass before he could get a look at me inside his domain, his garage.

Oops, too late.

"Who is that in my garage?" he demanded to know while coughing.

She told him to get back in the house. She was taking care of things.

He inched his way forward and paused, then bellowed, "No niggers allowed! No niggers allowed! I thought I could trust cha, but I see I can't trust cha! Ya know my rule. I don't want no niggers touching my garage! Naw I can't trust cha!"

She told him to go back in the house before he had another stroke, but he ignored her. There was nothing she could do to reason with him.

"You know things are different these days, Dick. You just can't tell 'em who to send out. Ya just gotta accept who they send. He's just doing his job. Let him finish. You know we've been needing that new door hung!"

She had real tears welling up behind her glasses, in her pale blue eyes. I felt sorry for her.

I told her she had done nothing wrong, but I had to leave. I began reloading my truck.

If I hadn't left right then and there, there's no telling what would have jumped off. I could imagine ole boy whipping out a hidden sawed off, and blowing my head off, then claiming either stroke-related dementia or swearing I threatened him or his wife's life. She'd have to go along with whatever he said or risk getting her own head blown to bits.

Either way, he wouldn't have even been handcuffed, let alone spend one night in jail, not that it would help me any after I lay dead from "trespassing" in his garage. When I reported in at work, my boss told me not to worry about it, he'd schedule me for a similar-paying job.

He offered me a half-hearted apology. I just nodded.

He said he wouldn't be sending anyone else out to that address. Instead of them being able to take advantage of the newspaper coupon, they'd have to call another higher-priced company, hopefully, for the missus's sake, a White installer.

CHAPTER 7

Witwe

Soon after moving to Houston, Texas, in late March, I filed my 1099 early in the morning at a H&R Block. Later that afternoon, I was sent to service a door in the exclusive area named the Woodlands. It was a gated senior complex with a guard.

The temp outside was ninety-eight degrees and climbing. I prided myself on attention to detail. My type of work benefitted by it.

The front yard was well maintained. There was a bad sky blue Cadillac sedan parked in the driveway.

The customer was an eighty-two-year-old German-born widow of a US airman, but man, she must have lived a charmed life, or had perfect genes, because she still looked good. Her face was smooth, with no deep wrinkles. She was a bottled blond who wore her hair cut short.

Nope, I wasn't personally attracted to her, but I do appreciate beauty when I see it. Since I hit fifty, I draw the line at sixty-year-olds who happen to still look classy, strutting a sexy walk, shapely, bigger butt, tiny waist, larger breasts, preferably with longer-looking hair, ideally in microbraids, my version of a real sexpot.

Her name was Elsa. Clearly, she still worked out. She told me how much she loved doing yoga. She was about five feet six inches, 140 pounds, everything in the right place.

She looked like a cross between Zsa Zsa and Ava Gabor. Red lipstick lit up her face's thinner upper and fuller lower lip.

To me, she sounded a lot like Ava on *Green Acres*. She told me she always wore dresses to show off her legs and, in the summer, sleeveless ones to showcase her firm arms.

I ain't mad at ha fa dat! When I came in for the payment, she offered me a cold drink and a comfy seat in her elegant silver and ivory living room.

Green silk plants were everywhere, but real live pink and white tulips in a big cut crystal vase pretty-upped a round glass-topped dining table. I accepted a bottle of chilled lemonade. She served it the right way, unopened, with a heavy-bottomed glass of clear ice.

Displayed on the marble mantel were two large framed photos, one of her and her husband taken for their fiftieth. The other one was of her husband in full dress uniform. There was an impressive collection next to it of his numerous brightly colored medals.

She relented they had never had children. I complimented her on a lovely home and for staying in such great shape. She was so doggone charming. I could see how someone could fall in love with her, especially when she was younger, no doubt a real fox.

She seemed to appreciate my conversation and blushed over the comment about her lasting good looks.

"I really miss my husband, William, (pronounced Wiljem), so very much. We were in love, married fifty-two years."

"Man, that was a lifetime! How did you two first meet?" I could tell he was her favorite subject.

She told me he was a lieutenant in the US Air Force. Her German group of girlfriends knew some of his friends and introduced them to each other. Several of the couples got married. Her military wedding was the last in the group before deployment to her desired destination, USA.

It was amusing to hear her describe secret chats she and her girls had when no men were around. When they all first arrived in the United States, the women had been talking among themselves about how they were attracted to Black men.

"American Blacks," she stressed.

Well, one day at a military ball, she put her foot in her mouth by speaking too freely:

"I love everyone. No matter what color!"

She was too regal for me to imagine her being all soused up, but she had to have been. Her husband's friends were insulted big time. They began protesting all at once.

"No, no, no, we don't like the Blacks over here, especially the men!"

"Remember, no to the Black man in America!"

So to drive home the point, she and her girls repeated, "No to the Black man in America!

Ta, ta, ta . . .," as if they were spitting from disgust.

Their little charade seemed to satisfy the men. Curious, I asked her, specifically how did her husband feel about the subject?

She said, "Oh, he did not care one way or the other. He used to say, 'I'm from Iowa, the quad cities.' But he'd go along with the rest of them to keep the peace. As long as he felt he could trust me, he was fine, and I never betrayed him with Black man or White."

I got ready to leave and thanked her for her hospitality.

She ended things with a curious statement: "It has been my pleasure talking with you. You know, one never really knows what good fortune awaits him right around the corner."

I thought for a second, then told myself, "Naw, you must be on the wrong track. Say goodbye now."

CHAPTER 8

Now I See

I've received more than my share of tips, from various races, during my career. The biggest tip until then was $50.00s cash money. I was paid a $100.00 dollar bill, by a middle-aged White guy who could not believe I could install his garage doors all by myself.

"Hey, buddy, who's going to help you install those two big doors?"

"Nobody, this is a one-man job."

"What? I gotta see this!"

With that, he pulled his lawn chair close enough to better see me, but not too close. He offered me a cold one he opened a bottle of Heineken from his wheeled cooler.

"When I'm all done, I'll take you up on a cold non-diabetic sweet tea."

He hunched his shoulders and pretended to jog inside the house, toting back a couple of bottles each of frosty sweet tea and sweating bottles of water. The temperature was a towering inferno of 115 degrees or so.

My box fan did absolutely nothing, so he brought out some new-fangled bladeless contraption which took things down to a much more tolerable 98 degrees or so. It was a routine install, nothing mind-blowing to figure out, but still I took my own sweet time in all that heat.

As always, I had my smooth jazz turned down low on my keep-me-company Bluetooth and tablet.

"There's nobody else out here, feel free to turn your music up, if you like."

"Thanks, but I'm used to it like this."

As soon as I completed the job, I got down and walked over to him for my pay and "cold one."

"Wow, I wouldn't have believed it if I hadn't seen it with my own two eyes! You know, you deserve some iced cold suds, don't you?"

"Thanks, but this hits the spot for me. I don't drink alcohol, but I could chase down this sweet tea with a cold bottled water though."

"Gosh I could have sworn that was at least a two-man job. Good I didn't bet, huh?"

I smiled and just said, "Yeah, guess so."

After I exchanged his credit card info for a receipt, he smugly beamed as he handed me a crisp bill with Ben Franklin's face on it.

"In this stifling heat, you sure did earn every penny of it! Great job!"

"Thanks a lot. I really appreciate it."

Firmly shaking his hand while looking him straight in the eye, I added, a la Denzel,

"My man!"

CHAPTER 9

"Yo', Daddy!"

I'll take every day of blistering heat to one twenty-four-hour period in the frigid tundra. I had frost bitten toes while serving in Anchorage. While working in Phoenix, my earliest assignment that day was to install a set of new lighter-weight custom doors. As usual, the heat was stifling, but the job wasn't going to do itself.

The doors were a wedding gift from the dad of the bride. He was paying for it and evidently overseeing the installation of the doors at her house while the honeymooners were off to Paris, France.

I knew immediately, by the scowl on his beefy, red, face, there would be a problem: me. He pulled up a chair as close as possible to the ladder on which I was standing.

I was steadily bombarded with inane questions and given unasked-for unwanted suggestions. After all, he was a retired military officer and retired engineer.

"What on God's green earth are you doing that for? That's not even necessary."

I told him, "I'd appreciate it, *sir*, if you would move your chair back, closer to the other side of the opening. Please give me room enough to work."

How dare I speak to him about anything!

"How are you going to install those big doors all by yourself? Where's your helper?"

He simply wouldn't accept the fact I didn't need a helper for residential doors, not even for the lighter, custom ones. He went on a rant, upping the volume with each insult.

"Look, I know, wherever you grew up, you didn't get a good education! I know your daddy left your family when you were young!"

In reality, little did this jerk off know or care that I grew up in a nurturing family environment, surrounded by a great work ethic by both parents, and most of the parents of other kids on the block. My dad was a union craftsman and my mom, a AAA headquarters, office secretary before becoming a RN. My siblings and I grew up reading in-house *Encyclopedia Britannica* and enjoying cultural enrichments, including regular treks to the neighborhood library and museums, and attending kiddy shows and age appropriate live concerts, (Michael and The Jacksons), but why bother wasting my breath trying to convince this yahoo of my worth?

"I know you didn't have the best training for this job!" I suppose he thought affirmative action got me the job, wrong!

Clearly, I desperately needed my pay that day. I told him, as nicely as I could, that if he really wanted the doors installed, he needed to back up out of the way.

"I'm going to my truck for a break."

I couldn't wait to get inside ole faithful, jack up the AC, gulp down a few cups of iced water, and call my boss to fill him in on this poster boy KKK wizard! He probably has his hood stashed somewhere in his own garage or, for sure, proudly displays his Confederate flag in plain public view in the privacy of his own home.

"Sieg Heil!"

I clicked my heels in my mind. My boss told me to just hurry and finish up the job and leave.

To which I said, "You're not here for this Oscar performance. I ask you to at least call him and tell him he must move away from right under my armpit, so I can work—the farther away, the better. I can barely think for his racist rants. He's keeping me from finishing this frickin' job!"

Be aware that my thirty-eight-year-old boss and I had a fairly good rapport. He said his best friend growing up was Black, not as in "some of my best friends are Black."

I said maybe this one requires the "big boss man's" touch because "clearly, I'm not the one he dreamed would be installing these doors!"

As soon as we hung up, I could hear the ring of a cell phone in the garage. The irate customer answered and began pacing back and forth like a caged big cat. He became more wound up, angrier and louder each step he took.

I was shocked when I returned. He had moved a few feet out but never stopped running that big ignorant mouth of his.

I felt like saying, "Look, joker, I know the world revolves around you and only you. Just let me finish and get the hell outta here!"

Upon resuming the job, I turned up my headphones and trudged on through, completing the job and transacting the business when done. Deep thinker that I am, is it any wonder that every single Black-looking person, especially Black men in America, aren't stroking out or "I'm comin', Elizabeth"-ing their chests from high-blood-pressure-caused heart problems, considering all the unnecessary added stress from living while Black in America? And N-O, I'm not going back to no Africa now that my pure genes have been diluted, thanks to multi-European slave traders, masters and overseers, despicable African potentates, and even the then-renowned world church sanctions.

The dilution of my blood can be attributed to mixing untold types of European and Native American blood and only God knows what else!

Not that I mind my Native brothers. My great-grandma's grandma was half-Negro and half-Cherokee, for real.

My Native bros and I can commiserate on Euro-dominance. They had their lands taken away from them, and we were taken away from our land. Bet they're sorry their ancestors, the original human beings, were too nice and hospitable to those fork-tongued White devils, many convicts, daring to darken their tepees.

It's no coincidence that, thanks to the US circulation of demeaning media, racial propaganda, and foreign word of mouth, most, if not all, immigrants, especially Black groups now "coming to America," arrive convinced they are superior to us homegrown Black folk, America's original builders. My personal encounters with customers from other countries who actually observe me working, seem in awe, and are driven to tell me to my face,

"Oh, you are such a hard worker."

Yes, I am grateful to have been born in America, in spite of her not living up to her ideals, specifically when it comes to my people, African Americans, the contributors of its base economies: king cotton, sugar cane, tobacco. You bet there is still a definite need to celebrate African American-Black History Month 365 days a year, every year, until US systemic racism is abolished!

That needs to be a global objective, but I'm mainly concerned about right here in the good ole USA, "land of the free, home of the brave." Just ask Crispus Attacks all about it, among so many other self-sacrificing US Blacks! I may as well finish my rant.

Let's just nationalize Juneteenth Day, June 19, while we're at it. Yeah, make it a bona fide American holiday to be celebrated by *all* Americans, flying a unified Ole Glory!

Unlike *all* other races, except the original Americans, Native Americans, my people never asked to be chained and hauled transatlantic in subhuman conditions in the first place! Don't dare tell me how today's Whites had nothing to do with enslaving my poor ancestors when until this day, every Caucasian in the United States is still benefitting by the entitlements granted by law and understood by all!

That said, pass reparations, and pass them *now* while you're at it! And I don't mean for paying to send me off to some college.

Like all other disenfranchised groups, we are entitled (that's right: entitled!) to decide what we wish to do with our own cash money so very long overdue. My people have been contributing to building this country with their blood, sweat, tears, and very lives since 1619, but show me where that is in my history book! For that matter, point out where it mentions the Black woman who John Glenn trusted to help him, be the first human to orbit around the earth! Katherine Johnson and her 2 Black female associates: Mary Jackson and Dorothy Vaughn! How I wish I could have met Malcolm while he was alive. I agree with a lot of his beliefs, especially with those he and Dr. King shared about addressing the U.N. about reparations on behalf of US Blacks. We all see what happened to both of them. Later the phenomenal Johnny Cochran, attorney at law, reportedly also had such plans before he mysteriously died of a brain aneurysm. Don't tell me about conspiracy theories either, after it was "real-news" reported Clinton's right hand Black man, appointed Secretary of Commerce, Ron Brown, ended up with a bullet behind his skull on a flight which killed everybody on that plane, just to get rid of him.

Where did I learn that fact, certainly not in any school book. I am a huge fan of Youtube's renowned Dr. Claud (no e) Anderson, check him out sometime, if you're really interested in learning something positive, and true about us African Americans.

Meanwhile, White people, pretend you're a compassionate human, the way indigenous people were to your ancestors.

Alright "Rev"! (Al) I hear you!

"Get your knee off our necks!"

Crush racism once and for all, it's within your power, but requires a total change in not only mindset, but heart. Of course, I have sense enough to know that can't happen until there is a paradigm shift in the general public; for sure by the time the US census reads "other/mixed" next to most citizen's names, in another half century or so, or for all of you self-avowed Christians", quoting my Ma, "…until Jesus returns!" In the meantime, as the world turns, allow our country's foundational documents to finally come to full fruition for one and all of America's legalized citizens!

Look I never considered myself any sort of advocate: for Blacks or females, but I do have many dynamic, female relatives, I care about who all deserve equal rights and pay, so at the same time, while you're at it, let's get rid of sexism and all the other vile isms damning our land, and this entire globe, to hell!

CHAPTER 10

Dry Wall

I seemed to run into quite a few old vets in AZ. This one particular guy was a retired colonel in the Marines. He had a deep tan, good physique and jarhead buzz cut. He looked to be in his late seventies or early eighties.

I was sent to his home to install dual garage door openers. I found that whoever installed the original ones had done a jackleg job. I shared my opinion with him, only to spur him on to share how great and thorough of a job he always did when working.

In other words, quit bellyaching and cut to the chase and finish doing the job the right way. As I tried to remove the mechanisms, the old drywall crumbled away, and I am not a dry wall installer.

And why did I say that?

"I don't know what you think you're doing! Oh, ya doing it all wrong!

I thought, "You claim to be such a genius, why haven't you done it by now yourself?" But I never said a word.

He kept inching closer to me, high up on my ladder, raising his voice with each step. I felt it best to give my boss a call.

He agreed to call the colonel and instruct him to back off so I could finish. I tried figuring it out, how to tackle such a job not covered on YouTube.

When done, I asked the customer what did he want to do next. Did he want to speak with my boss or what?

He gave a smirky smile and said, "Everything's great, *buddy.*"

He even patted me on my sweaty back and insisted on giving me a cold drink, which he popped open out of my sight prior to handing it to me. Ole Miss Jane Pittman and grown Celie in The Color Purple, came to mind.

He said he'd "take care of things."

After loading up my truck to leave, I watched the colonel from the end of the driveway as he mounted his ladder, climbed to the garage ceiling, and pulled down wires and dry wall. Later my boss told me that customer called me everything but the "bad word".

My boss also said he told the ole coot, no, I won't be able to come out there until the end of next week. That was why I was allowed the chance to try to fix it first, lucky me.

I've learned, over the course of twenty years, as hard as ya try, ya' can't win 'em all. So don't kick yourself, just chalk some things up to human nature and all that White privilege.

Ya' know, living alone allows me to do whatever I enjoy doing, not watching much TV, preferring to spend most of my free time on my pc, playing chess and going on social media. I share Netflix with my mother in another state, she loves historical documentaries.

Speaking of media, one of my FB former classmates from elementary raves over the TV show; *Black-ish.* She insists her two favorite episodes: Juneteenth & Hope, should be pre-empting the needless nonsense often on news channels. I only mention it here because I've never heard anyone so geeked up over anything on TV, understandably since original Roots.

CHAPTER 11

When You Do For The Least Of These

PART 1
Fallen between the Cracks

My job sent me way out in the boonies of Phoenix to estimate the cost of a repair. I replaced two springs for the customer's old rickety garage. It was too heavy for the elderly widow to lift by herself.

The poor little thing was around eighty-five, White, short, with a Dowager's hump and sparse white hair. Her husband of sixty years had died a few years earlier.

They had two sons. Neither of whom came by to even check on their own mother because she refused to sell the property and give them a cut.

Mama chose to, instead, abide by Papa's wishes—to keep holding on to the property. "Never ever sell!"

She told me the old farm sat on two acres, and a lot of old farm equipment remained where he last left it. I replaced the door springs but told her I couldn't do a thing about installing a remote because it seemed she had no working electricity in the garage.

She admitted the lights had been off for quite some time. She had been using a kerosene lamp to read books by at night.

She must have had a bad infection because as she passed by me, my sensitive nose got a full "pouf" out from under her swishing Little House on the Prairie dress, which let me know there was most likely no running water as well. Man! How on earth was this lady surviving?

I asked her if she belonged to a church, and she answered yes. I suggested she confide in someone she trusted at her church, like her pastor maybe, letting him know her bad circumstances, so she could get help finding a honest realtor.

I did say, "You know, you could get a lot of money for this property and the machinery stored in the barn. Most of this outside stuff is so badly rusted. You aren't in any shape to be trying to take care of all this by yourself. Ma'am, I'm not trying to hurt your feelings, I can see you've been trying hard to take care of things all alone, but can't you see? You don't have to. Your front door is overgrown with bushes, and I can see a tree growing through your roof! Look at that big bandage on your leg."

She said she had hurt herself trying to cut down the bushes which had overtaken her front door. The only way in and out was through her back door, and trees had grown up all around her house, causing it to slant to one side.

There was no sense in her suffering all alone out of a sense of duty to a dead husband who should have never made such a hard and fast rule in the first place. He knew she was used to obeying his orders.

Investors had built a community of estate homes up the road costing big bucks, so her property would have gotten her a pretty penny, more than enough for her to live comfortably on. Not being privy to all the intricate details prevented me from going any farther.

So much was going on wrong, I never got to ask how was she able to schedule my visit. She was so lonely and looked so pitiful my heart went out to her, but when she stubbornly turned down my offer to call somebody else to help her, she said sadly, "No, there is no one else to call."

Reluctantly, I had to leave.

Part 2

Elder Neglect

Now I may not be a Bible-thumping churchgoer, but like my mother reminds me, "Stop pretending you never accepted Jesus!" I can truthfully say I do believe in the golden rule, and "What goes around, comes around." I've been told I phrase it that way to keep from saying the scripture it is based on. "You reap what you so." Either way, it's true.

I've personally been through tough times, so I know firsthand what it feels like to be homeless and hungry. Those low points have softened my heart for the down and out, at least for needy females.

I figure a man is a man, with or without missing limbs. There is always something a man can do for a buck or a meal, barring severe mental issues.

Face it, our government has gutted the hell outta humanity in our country, especially mental illness. There are no more safety nets.

There have been far too many victims to list here, but these are my main examples of charity, in no certain order.

I got a call post-Hurricane Harvey to repair a garage door system. A Houston White lady in her late eighties let me in. I've found that these elderly White mostly widows must really fear being put in a home because when they live on the outskirts of town, all alone, they seem to prefer toughing it out in the wilderness, over being in a old folks' home. She seemed a bit confused. When I'd say something, she'd sometimes give unrelated answers, but I didn't feel her hearing had anything to do with it.

I could see her bedroom from the living room. She wandered into her bedroom, searching for something.

The bed was floating around in moldy, smelly water. It looked like someone had been sleeping in it.

I asked was she sleeping in that bed, and she said, "Yes, where else would I sleep?"

When I tried to explain I couldn't make repairs until the garage electricity came back on, she changed the subject. I asked her who else lived there, and she said in a real frail voice, "I live all alone. I'm eighty-six years old and have outlived my whole family, my husband died before our two girls, and they both died in their fifties!"

As she spoke, she kept wading through the yucky water. Twice, I heard something plop in the water followed by what looked like a long tail.

She couldn't help the stench coming from below her private parts. The dirty water tapped it down a bit, but before she went in the bedroom, I nearly lost my breakfast.

I kept emergency Social Services numbers on speed dial to report elder neglect and abuse. When I said they needed to hurry and rescue her, the lady answering the phone told me, "Sir, there are thousands of stranded little old ladies living alone. We can only do what we can do as soon as we can." She then took my information.

I hated telling the customer I couldn't repair her unit but told her I'd called her some help and I hoped they would get there real soon. I tried talking her out of going in that bedroom but didn't want to scare her too much, so I just said, "There are live critters swimming in that dirty water. You might wanna sleep on your nice, dry couch in the front room and stay outta there, okay?"

She nodded yes, saying she would. When I asked was there anyone else I could call for her, she told me there was no one else.

I didn't want to leave her alone and felt bad, but after doing what little I could do, I dreaded pressing on to five other stops, no telling what I'd fine.

PART 3

House Arrest

I made a trip out to give an estimate for a door install at another White widow's house back in Phoenix. She was in her mid-eighties, also living all alone.

Her mind was sharp, but she was physically frail. Was I ever shocked on the next day when I returned to do the install.

When she answered the door, I asked, "What in the world happened to you? Yesterday you looked just fine."

"I fell face down, trying to step out of the tub, and couldn't catch myself."

She had broken her left leg. It was in a cast, and she used a quad cane to get around.

Her little face looked like a young Mike Tyson had gone five rounds on it. How in the world did she call for help? Maybe she wore one of those devices. I didn't see a phone.

They weren't commonplace back then, but man, did she ever need one of those step-in tubs or simply a walk-in shower, except most women prefer a good bubble bath. I told her how sorry I was for all she'd been through. I gave her a gentle shoulder hug. She seemed to melt away.

I offered to call anyone she wanted me to, but she told me a home aide was coming out sometime soon that day, which was music to my ears. I asked her was she in pain. She said not exactly. She had taken a pill with her microwave breakfast. She didn't want to get "hooked."

Her biggest need seemed to be companionship. There was a country gospel show playing loudly on TV.

She had tears brimming up in her eyes as I left. I gave her a little embrace around her shoulders.

I felt bad I couldn't sit until the aide arrived but did what I could—prop her leg up and handed her a cold bottled water from the fridge before saying, "Don't worry, I'm sure the aide will be here real soon. You be more careful, okay?"

She nodded, looking so pitiful.

"If you can, get a step-in shower, okay? She nodded yes. Goodbye now."

PART 4

Homeless in the Hood

My Saturday workday was done, and I was on my way home when I happened to pass an older-looking homeless Black lady trying to get her over stuffed cart up under the overpass. She looked to be in her late sixties but had lived a hard life. Suddenly, a monsoon stormed down outta nowhere. She let go of her packed cart, raised both arms, and let out the most bloodcurdling, soul-searing primal wail I'd ever heard; not even in my military days had anyone sounded so wounded. It was as if she had given up on life and wouldn't be long for this world.

I said out loud, "Man, is she in rough shape!"

Like Superman, I made a quick U-turn and pulled over to the curb and parked. About a half an hour passed before I was finally able to convince her to let me help her.

She refused to get on the passenger side until I first bench-pressed all she had to her name—that loaded stinking cart into my truck. I have a sensitive nose and unintentionally frowned as I helped her into the passenger seat.

She told me, "Look, I know I stank, but what cha expect? I don't know when I last bathed. So I'm sorry. Thanks for picking me up though."

I told her not to worry, that I was driving her to my place, out of all the rain, where she could clean up, catch her breath, and eat some good ole home cookin'. She said nothing, but a look of calm came over her face.

I lived in a small one-bedroom apartment alone, just the way I like it. I showed her the restroom and handed her a clean bath towel and a couple of washcloths. There was a neutral body wash in the tub-shower stall. I kept a box of Arm & Hammer soda on the vanity for added toothpaste oomph when needed, and there was a green bottle of rubbing alcohol with Epsom salts ready to be poured in a steamy, hot, soaking tub.

House cleaning supplies were beneath the sink. I tapped on the door and told her to put her things in the trash bag I gave her and tie it up so I could toss it.

I told her to take her time. I'd be right back from the dollar store two blocks away. I said I was getting her some new stuff to wear. She volunteered her favorite color was blue. I bought her one navy and one purple jogging outfit, white canvas gym shoes, a three-pack of panties, and hygiene items: a tiny Secret, a pink toothbrush and some paste, a small big-tooth comb and a brush, a bar of Dial, a mirrored compact, and tiny jar of Vaseline for ash.

I got a good vibe off her; so as expected, when I got back, she was still singing along with the radio, this time to Patti LaBelle's Over the

Rainbow. Nothing looked disturbed or missing. I hung her "goodie bag" on my side of the door and let her know it was there. She got outta the tub to see what I had bought her, reaching her hand out around the knob.

When she came out of the bathroom, she had the big towel wrapped around her head. She was clean-smelling, looking a little refreshed. I could tell she was feeling her Cheerios all dressed in her new, navy outfit. I figured she had scrubbed the hell outta my loofa, but I could always replace that. I felt like one proud papa.

I peeped inside. She had left everything spic and span, cleaner than I had.

She called herself Icie, age 67. She had been married a long time ago, but when she lost her job at the plant and came down with breast cancer, her younger husband left her, and since she had no close kin or real friends, she ended up homeless.

She said she'd tried several shelters, but the folks in 'em were worse off than she was. I had made a stock pot full of tasty, real meaty, all-ground beef and Italian sweet sausage spaghetti with a ton of cheese. I'd ate my fill and was planning on freezing the rest after eating more that day, but instead, I slowly heated it all up, fixed her and myself a heaping bowl each, plus garlic bread. I told her to help herself to the rest.

I set out some chilled bottled water and two cans of soda, Coke and Red Pop, telling her to take her pick. "Now don't be shy." I ended up with the Coke.

She then said she liked hot coffee, no matter how hot it was outside. I told her I only drank cocoa, so she accepted that. She almost inhaled the leftovers, which were enough to fill up three starving lumberjacks. It did me good, though, to see her swallow her food but hoped she wouldn't choke on it. Just in case, I went over the

Heimlich in my head and told her so. A remnant of a girlish smile crossed her face. It was getting dark, so I told her she could sleep on my love seat. She was short enough to fit it. I handed her a clean folded pair of sheets and a light blanket, plus bed pillow from the coat closet top shelf. I liked keeping my AC on good and supercool.

I went to bed. You may wonder was I worried, having a rank stranger, albeit female, under my roof, but nope. I kept certain protective gear handy. I felt safe.

She let me take the lead without complaint, not a word when I told her in the morning we'd find her a "good" shelter. Sunday was a sunny, dry, off day. We drove through McDonald's for a sausage biscuit with cheese and egg, hash browns, and OJ.

True to form, she also said she'd like some coffee, if that was okay. I didn't mind ordering her a cup with three sugars and two creams and told her so. Our first stop was at a inner-city church, but it had way too many rules and regulations. The head of the urban churches must not have heard one of my favorite quotes by Dr. King: "Christianity must be a head light, not a tail light." I told her not to worry, we'd find the perfect spot for her. I then drove her way out in the suburbs to a huge Mormon church complex, and man, what a difference, as night and day! Their only stipulations were if a needy person agreed to spend the night in their two-person bunk bed dorm, you had to keep your area and own body neat and clean, and attend mandatory daily Mormon religious studies. They probably had used clean clothes to give out because there were plenty of different types of White addicts all over the place. If you refused the classes, then they fed you, allowed you to spend that one night, but you had to *vamos* that next morning.

My little lady agreed to stay and follow the rules. I was happy for her and proud of her in her strange, new surroundings.

She couldn't thank me, "and the good Lord" enough and gave me a peck on the cheek as we said our goodbyes. It felt great knowing I'd made a positive difference in her life.

My mind revisited those tough times when I was homeless or living out of my car and starvin', bathing at the Y. I hope she was able to get the help she really needed and deserved and used it to turn her life around. I guess the Mormons help folks get jobs and training or GED guidance, whatever; anything beats the way she was when I happened to run across her.

PART 5

Midwest Sistah

When I moved to get a promotion, relocating from Houston to San Antonio, I found a nice, affordable townhouse to buy in "Mexicali" town, where no one bothers me or my vehicles, perfect. Unlike back in good ole Houston, I now had to search for the hidden homeless. I guess I'd become a type of strange addict. Every now and then I'd come across a single Black lady huddled under a overpass but few and far in between compared to Harris County where a bunch of males with a sprinkling of female homeless could be found everywhere in the inner city. Social workers from colder states sent theirs down on a one-way Greyhound ticket, whether sane or insane.

Based on the hot, humid climate, I knew there had to be a bunch of homeless somewhere in town. I found myself searching for a big part missing from my day, feeding the homeless, once I was settled in; I did happen across one homeless village by accident.

I felt like the 70's Black TV detective, Tenafly. San Antonio's law enforcement does a great job of policing to keep them hidden, far away from the tourists' eyes.

Driving home from work, in the pouring rain, I picked up yet another homeless, Black lady. She looked early sixties having lived a hard life.

She wasn't nearly as hard to get in my truck. She went by Barbie, yes, as in Ken's doll, age 62, from Harvey, Illinois.

Her older sister helped move her down out of an abusive situation, but then she was killed herself by who knows, her body left out on her back porch, in the rain. One thing led to the next, and before you knew it, ole Barb was homeless.

I figured there was a lot of her story left out, but I didn't nose around further. I told her I would take her to my place if that was okay, "no strings."

I turned on the heat to knock off the chill since she was soaked and wet and shivering. She gave me that look, then said, "Yeah, okay. Thanks for stoppin'. Do you have a cigarette or a joint?"

"Nope, don't smoke."

Swinging by the nearby dollar store, I told her to "sit tight" while I removed my keys and went in. "I'll be right back." It only took me a few minutes to do my mini-shopping spree for my new house guest.

On the way home, I went through the drive-through and picked us both up some Whataburger meals. She asked for hot coffee instead of pop. No problem.

I shared my usual MO of taking her to a nearby shelter first thing in the morning, if she liked. She quickly told me she did not like.

I asked if she wanted to take a shower or not, and she said she'd like that. When we got to my place, I showed her the bathroom with shower and handed her a big towel and two washcloths and her goody bag with one, medium green sweat suit. I didn't pick up as good a vibe from her.

When I instructed her to throw her filthy things in a plastic bag to toss out, she immediately let me know she wanted her things *washed*, which strangely made me smile, but I obliged her and still gave her the new stuff.

I laid out a set of clean sheets and blanket and pillow on the futon, her guest bed.

Later that evening, while watching TV, I could hear her guts growling and asked could she go for something else to eat?

"Yeah, why not? You must be hungry by now yo'self." For the first time, she sorta smiled.

I had made a big pot of chili with beans the day before. So I heated it up with day-old corn bread, loading up a couple of big bowls full. I joined her at the small kitchen table. I could tell she wasn't big on talking about her past or present situation, so no questions, beyond was she a native.

"Help yo'self." Again, I tried taking a stab at Southern hospitality.

"Thanks. Ya gotta cold beer?"

"Nope, don't drink, unless ya' talkin' about root beer."

A curious look crossed her face. She gobbled up every bit of her chili and asked anyway for seconds.

It was a nice sound, hearing her sopping the bread, and "umm umming" as she went.

I peacefully slept in my bed. Keep in mind, my size, six feet one inch, 250-pound frame, in fairly good shape, without obvious vices, might have caused these small women to think twice about trying something underhanded during the night. She slept wearing her new clothes in my "chill room", next to my master.

The next morning I drove us a block over to Burger King and ordered us each a turkey sausage and cheese egg biscuit with tots and OJ. She too wanted hot coffee, only black, which I bought.

I was surprised there was no comment from the peanut gallery, allowing me to order for her. Thank goodness, her cart was not as heavy as the first lady's.

She said she wanted to be on her way. "Thanks again," she said as she began eating her meal while pushing her cart on down the street.

No, no goodbye smooch. Glad I was able to help her out, and I wish her all the best.

PART 6

Homeless in "Mexicali"

On my way home from work one day, I had a taste for some juicy KFC and stopped by the one in my neighborhood. Back in Houston, I was used to the homeless, mostly cool breeze type Black dudes, messed up, ex-vets, and addicts with their hand out. Sometimes I'd slip them a little loose change, depending upon my mood.

A few females appeared now and then who I'd probably slip a couple of bucks, but not the men, no, never. Early on, I'd been taught a real man carries his own weight. Even a legless man could buck dance to earn a buck.

A older-looking White lady in her late seventies or so, stood in front of KFC with her cart to the side of the door. As I opened the door, she slipped in ahead of me.

Usually, I would have never ran into her, but there she stood staring me in the face. I went straight to the counter to order a carry-out while she asked for a cup of iced water.

The Hispanic young lady behind the counter looked irritated but served her. The next thing I knew, the old lady stood in the middle of the place screaming from the bottom of her heart and top of her lungs, "I'm hungry!" then even louder, "I'm sooo hungry! If anybody wants to help me, I'll be over by the window drinking my water."

Say what you will, but you had to admire her guts. She sat and loudly crunched on the ice.

Everyone else in the restaurant looked Hispanic. They all sat at their booths and tables, glaring at hungry ole girl, but nobody said one word, or made a move her way.

The dame in distress for some reason zeroed in on me, asking if I had any money. I told her no, but if she liked, I'd buy her a meal.

"Yes, I'd like a meal. Thank you."

I ordered my usual legs and thighs meal to-go and a three-piece KFC all-breast meal for her plus a big Sprite. She ripped that bag open and tore into one of those big chicken breasts like a woman possessed.

I thought to myself she really is starving. Before I left, I saw her scarf down the first one.

I had a mixed bag of feelings. On the one hand, it was sad to see an elderly woman of any race going hungry right here in the good ole USA.

Yet it was great to be able to feed a fellow American in need of a meal. All I know is, if I were filthy rich or politically connected, I'd hire the brightest minds, like a Brittney Exline or Bill Gates, to do something about America's hunger problem for all ages, sexes, and races. I'd coax them to lead a think tank on also solving the US homeless epidemic. Cutting out the mental hospitals didn't do a thing but add to and complicate the growing homeless problem.

Just think, I keep running into elderly women, so there has to be millions of unseen starving kids somewhere nearby. All of them can't be living in cars.

What has our once-rich-in-resources country come to?

PART 7

Homeless in A Car

My place is located at a intersection across from a no-named gas station. One typically sweltering "Mexicali" day, I could see from my front room window a raggedy big ole, black, broken-down Olds, stuck half way in and half out of the gas station lot.

When I later drove over for a weekly fill up, I saw seated inside of the car a heavyset Black lady, sweating like a mule. The temp was around 110 degrees outside and probably over 120 degrees inside that junky car.

I got myself a cold bottle of water, and her some Gatorade, a water and a lunchmeat snack box. When I bent down to hand her the bag, I got a good whiff of the reeking odors from inside that car. My mouth said nothing, but my face spoke volumes. "Good God! Oooh wee!"

The lady said, "Thanks, and yeah, I know my coochie stank! It's over two hundred degrees in here! I have no air and nobody to help me!"

I can still picture her face all twisted up and hopeless. There was barely enough room for her to squeeze behind the wheel. Junk was piled up to the ceiling in that back seat, and the passenger seat was full from the floor up.

She looked late fifties but had lived a hard life.

"What can I do to help you? Call an agency?"

She responded, "Sir, if you believe anyone will come to my aid, in this locality and heat, then by all means, please do contact that entity post haste!"

Say what? Now she had to have been a teacher, lawyer, or some sort of medicine woman in another life with that vocabulary.

I had to give it to her though. She was a ballsy broad for having the nerve to use such lingo right there in the heart of the hood in her terrible situation, sitting in such a ram-shackled vehicle.

I figured the Red Cross, Salvation Army, or Catholic services could help her, if they had room. It pissed me off how the inner-city churches had *sooo* many rules to qualify for tax exemptions but never enough to make a real difference in the lives of the homeless. Hell, I guess they do the best they can.

Why didn't she at least try taking a "Mary bath" in the laundry mat next door? They had a public toilet, but she may not have known about it.

Like the gas station, maybe the attendant would have just ran her back outside. Who knows?

On a hunch, I called the Salvation Army and let her talk for ten minutes on my cell. She thanked me for my help and even shed a tear or two.

I patted her on the shoulder and told her to think nothing of it, just know I was a firm believer in the golden rule, and I've been where she is. Later that evening, after running my Saturday errands, I was glad to see the car was no longer there.

Hopefully, she got the help she *sooo* badly needed.

PART 8

The Last of the Good Samaritan

It was early on a chilly, rainy Sunday. I made a U-turn to go by a breakfast joint on the opposite side of the street.

I noticed a tender tan, Black chick around my age, early fifties, just lying there under the overpass on a nasty, stained mattress. I thought what if she was my own mother or sister, so when I ordered my blowout breakfast, I also ordered her the exact same thing.

Driving back across to deliver her surprise meal drug up flashbacks of my own Oliver Twist tale. Smiling big, and wanting nothing in return; I walked up to her and proudly presented my goodwill gift.

She stared at me, stood up, smiled, took the food, removed the clear plastic cover, and said, "Ahhh, isn't that sweet of you?"

Then she proceeded to smack me in the face, *Soupy Sales-Three Stooges* style, with the uncovered plate of hot food and smeared the dripping plate down the front of my shirt. The plate, by the way, contained hot grits, cheese eggs, sausage gravy, bacon, and one buttered pancake with syrup, plus two cartons of OJ.

Her swan song to me was this: "I don't accept nothin' from no MFing niggas!" Was she color blind and crazy?

I can't begin to put into words how much I felt like stompin' her crazy head in! Thank goodness, my cooler head prevailed, and I bent down to salvage the intact OJs from the ground and vowed never to help another homeless off-her-meds wench ever again.

That vow has since proven to be temporary.

CHAPTER 12

Creepiest Customers

PART 1
S&M Success

Mrs. Gump sure had the right idea: "Life is like a box of chocolates . . ." You never know what you're dealing with until you arrive at the assigned address.

Such was the case with one of my creepiest customers. A repair was needed at the mansion of a customer who looked like Lurch and spoke like Bela Lugosi's Dracula.

He lived in a sprawling estate complete with a huge infinity pool and a couple of cabanas out back, amidst palm trees. He welcomed me into his inner sanctum, an elaborately-built garage.

Before I started working, he proudly showed off several of his favorite S&M inventions, the key to his fortune. I'd never seen or heard of anything like them before.

You could tell a lot of ingenuity went into creating them. They sure looked expensive, but I am not at liberty to describe them to you.

Let's just say he became extremely wealthy through his unique, some would say perverted, ideas. He was the type of guy I could imagine saying to himself about me, "You better be glad your job knows where you are working."

Imagine that being said to you, all alone, in Dracula's voice, restrained in his grand garage.

Scary.

PART 2

The Fetish

For a brief time, I had my own private business. I felt I owed it to myself and my ancestors to at least try my hand at being a real self-made bi'nessman.

It was during that time I went to service the door of another of my creepiest customers. This customer lived at the dead end of the street. His driveway was slanted, and if someone wanted to peep in his garage, they would have to walk back to it. You couldn't see it straight from the street or sidewalk, which struck me as odd.

Who knows what he's hiding? This guy was a milk chocolate-colored, myopic, six feet seven inches, around three-hundred-pound man, who weirdly kept slinking up behind me while I was up on the ladder. You'll be hard pressed to guess why.

It creeped me out at first. I told him I needed him to step away and stop putting his face up my crack! The second time, I demanded to know what the hell was wrong with him. Why did he keep sticking his nose up my ass?

He gave me a sheepish grin and, in hushed tones, confessed, "Oh, I'm sorry. I have a flatulence fetish."

I was so disgusted. I looked down in his face and cursed him out, telling him if he didn't step away and stay away, I would not finish the job, and he *would* pay me for my time!

The whole time, if need be, I planned on either cracking his thick skull with my claw hammer dangling from my tool belt or slashing his face with my trusty, razor-sharp box cutter. He may have hoped I'd let go of a squeeze out, but he was sadly disappointed. The last thing I wanted to do was make his day. (Harry/Clint)

For some reason, I was more suspicious of him tackling me than I had been of Dracula. You know my number one "creepie" had to be that hologram guy. "Eek, eek, eek!"

Oh, the life of a Black garage door guy. I gotta million stories, but I'm only sharing the best of the best with lucky you.

CHAPTER 13

360

Recently, I was assigned a job to install three custom doors, same garage. After taking measurements, it was clear whoever built the garage did not do so precisely.

In other words, it would be necessary for the garage door install guy, me, to somehow further customize the door openings. I had learned to call the boss out as soon as a problem presented itself.

He came, he saw, he said, "Just do your best."

In the end, I asked the customer was he satisfied, and he said he was. A few days later, I got a call-back to that same address.

Only the first door really fit. The other two, with ill-fitting casings, were noticeably noisy.

My boss was summoned once again, and unexpected by me, the warehouse distributer also showed up. At first, when he thought my White boss was the installer, he calmly reassured the owner, "There is no need to worry. We'll get everything straightened out."

During the conversation, when the rep asked my boss, "Ames, exactly when did you do this job?" he was told that my boss did not do the install, but me, "my guy," Joe Blow did it two days ago.

With that intel, the supplier snatched out his cell and pulled up my Black employee ID, and it was off to the races. His demeanor made a 360.

"My God! Good Lord, how in the hell could anybody mess up this job like this?"

I watched as his body language became agitated, his face turned beet red and contorted, and I heard his tone change from confident to irate, all totally inappropriate in front of the customer. No matter what, those representing the company should always follow the unspoken rule of remaining professional at all times, and sound in complete control while in front of the paying or prospective customer.

So you tell me, what on earth could have caused this guy's whiplash in personality after seeing my Black face on his cell? My boss later told me in confidence that he knew I could do better, and he expected as much when I'd have to return later in the week to "make it work!"

Since he put it to me like he did, I had to agree. Guess what happened then?

That rep was so angry over finding out who I was, and what I'd done, he inquired about all my other jobs for the company and my boss. I don't know if he knew my boss called each customer within a week after the job was done to check for customer satisfaction, so he wasn't concerned to hear of the inquiry about my work history.

When all was said and done, come to find out, my average was in the 90s; the grounds for dismissal was in the 70s. I got a call one morning from my boss soon after redoing the job. He left a one-word message: "Congratulations!"

When I got off work, I called him and asked what did the one-word message mean? Congratulations for what exactly?

He said that guy must have assumed since that one job wasn't done right, then most likely there were many others done wrong. He put in for a official inquiry about my work history with them.

Imagine his surprise to learn of my overall averages. The congratulations was for my new raise in pay, a certain amount for regular installation and double that for certain custom jobs with more difficulty.

Sure, I know, without asking, my boss would get his cut first, but so what? Didn't he hire me sight unseen, over the phone, while recognizing my male African American voice? Hadn't he treated me fairly despite racial differences? Yes to all the above.

Talk about a negative turned into a positive, receiving such great news boosted my mood to on top of the world!

Update: Several months later what my positive boss thought was under his control backfired and through another way, that vindictive fart found a way to stop doing business with my bosses' company after all.

Thankfully there were more fish in the sea.

Chapter 14

"Oh Lordy"

Have you ever heard of Ysleta, Texas? I hadn't either before being sent there for a small install. My GPS sent me around in circles, so I stopped a cop and asked for directions. He only gave me generalities.

Finally, a county road worker gave me more specific instructions, which led me to the right address, way out in nowhere, to a big ole farm. The elderly White couple came out together to greet me. It was amazing, to me, they seemed to be still living there just the two of them. Maybe they had a not visible to me at the time, live in helper. When I got a good look behind their home, off in the distance were tiny bunk houses. I guessed their farmhands or field hands lived in them, maybe illegals. None of my business.

They looked in their late eighties. After showing me the garage, the husband went back inside the house and resumed watching his baseball game. His sight line allowed him to see me and I him from the living room window to the garage entrance. I brought my tablet and trusty Bluetooth, first playing some vintage Johnny Taylor: "Whose making love . . ." I thought it may have been a little too loud and racy for my surroundings and started to turn it down a bit as I pulled up one of my all time, favorite mood-lifters, Steve Martin in *The Jerk*. The song "Ole Lordy, Pick a Bale a Cotton" came on, and I couldn't resist chiming in.

The lady owner told me, "No, no, no, leave it turned up! I love this song! It reminds me of back on my daddy's farm, when Mother and I used to sit on the porch, sipping lemonade, enjoying ah, ah, your people singing those type a songs. Boy, those sure were the good ole days when everybody loved each other! Why can't it be like that now?"

I knew the song by heart and sang it a la Steve's way, clowning around, and to my surprise, the little thin lady came back inside the garage just a-singing. Well, not really. She spoke the words and held up her skinny arms, swaying the top of her body, not the bottom half. She looked so happy. She began dancing a jig, her tiny feet just a-movin'. Wow! Was I ever surprised!

Taking her cue, I jumped down from my ladder and joined in, singing and moving just like the jerk.

"Jump down turn around, pick a bale a cotton!"

Our voices blended like any Hootin' Annie. There was a part she didn't know, but I did, and so in a good mood, I decided to bust a move and gently fell down on my knees on top of some cardboard.

"Get down on my knees!"

You would have thought Elvis did a split right in front of her.

"Oh! Oh! Oh! You sure do know the whole song, and you're a good dancer like, ah, your people back on Daddy's farm!" She was *soooo* happy, happy, happy!!!

Ordinarily, I wouldn't coon it up for all the tea in China, but this lil' lady was so full of joy and liveliness, she honestly touched my heart, and I couldn't help myself but to humor her and join in the good ole-fashioned fun. Now if she had been closer to say sixty, that *never* would have happened, but as fate had it, she looked shy of ninety, and so it did me all the good in the world to see her smile big and be so animated for her age. She shared how her caregiver (or "Mammie") Magnolia took such good care of her as a child. She said, "they loved her like family" and ole Magnolia "treated her like her very own."

I could imagine poor Magnolia cuddling missy while telling her own child to go sit down some where, being forbidden to handle both at the same time.

"Wow! You enjoy your music just like ah, ah, your people did way back then!"

Mind you, even *if* that sweet lil' ole White lady had slipped up and said *the bad word*, considering her age and generation, I would have ignored it, pretending I hadn't even heard it.

"I can tell your mother raised you right."

"Thank ya, ma'am, I'll be sure and tell her ya said so."

"Oh, she's still alive?"

"Yes, ma'am."

"Now see what you just said? I knew you were raised right! Well, please tell her she did a fine job raising you."

"Thank ya again."

"Are you from Texas? Ya don't sound like it."

"No'me" (a la "Hoke" Driving Miss Daisy).

"I'm from Detroit, Michigan."

"Oh. I sure wish people today were as loving as they once were. I sure do miss those good ole days!"

You could tell she was pining for her heavenly childhood. Nostalgia aside, my guts began growling. I asked her where was the closest place for me to grab something to eat?

Pointing up the road, she said, "About forty miles that a way."

She offered me a cold drink from the fridge in the garage. I accepted a chilled apple juice from a six pack.

"Thank ya, ma'am."

She volunteered to "rustle" me something up from the chock full a mostly meat chest freezer next to the fridge. She held it opened for me to see inside, but I at first declined.

"Oh, I know you don't want me to cook you anything."

I peeped over in the opened chest and saw a big supreme pizza and asked if she would mind heating that up for me.

She said, "Of course not!" and baked it in the real oven, I think to also have me stick around just a little longer.

I sincerely thanked her. Once done with my food, I prepared to pack up and leave. Her parting words sounded so familiar, with few exceptions. Most times I left an elderly White customer's home; the women almost always did and said the same thing.

First, they'd wag that finger at me, followed by "You be careful now and stay outta trouble," usually said with a wry smile, if not a twinkle in the eye. Unsure, maybe they told their own sons that same thing before they left home, but I seriously doubt it. Just before I left, she went back in the house, to her bedroom, and came back out with something tightly balled up in her hand. She took my hand and thrust the something into mine and quickly closed my hand up around whatever it was, as if I wasn't to look at it until I'd left. Hubby was still enjoying his ball game.

As she closed my hand, she whispered, "Something for the missus and the little ones."

I took a before and after photo of the job and sent it to my boss, my new routine to help cover myself. Before starting up my truck, I opened my hand. Guess what was in it? I know, but how much? There were five crisp $100 bills crumpled up together!

My mouth dropped open! Oh, I nearly forgot, *and* she gave me a rave review to my boss over the phone, telling him she wished *all* her repairmen were just like me, nice, polite, and friendly, doing a great job. He thanked her for taking the time to chat with him about her opinion of my finished work.

According to ole Big Unk T, "Now ya can't beat that with a stick, but you sho' can take it straight to the bank!"

CHAPTER 15

Close Encounters

When my Army stint was up in California, I decided to relocate elsewhere, following a really messy divorce from my first wife, a civilian and mother of my beloved son. The new girl in my life had been in the Army, but in a different platoon. Once out, she joined her folks in Queens, New York.

She was a naturalized US citizen, hailing from Nassau, Bahamas. She was a knockout, dark, very shapely, five feet ten inches of Amazon goddess, highly motivated, intelligent, but I later found out she was also very indecisive. We chose to "Jump the broom" at the Justice of the Peace; followed by sharing a unbelievable week of sheer ecstasy in Belize! We enjoyed such marital bliss; although the honeymoon proved to be over in just shy of six months…sadly, ending in a annulment.

Through her family connections, I was hired on, in security, at one of the most prestigious investment firms in Manhattan. I sported a blazer at work.

It was a busy place with many visits from political bigwigs whose security details shut the place down for obvious reasons. Just a few of the who's who during working hours were: Bill and Hill, Gen. Colin Powell, and Cheney.

"Very interesting."

On one of my off days, my girl and her mom invited me to join them on a day trip to, of all places, a tony part of Connecticut. Her older sister was a nanny for a filthy rich Jewish couple.

I accepted, not wanting to be home all day alone, without my "Brown Suga." The husband was a middle-aged guy, personable, downright friendly, yet super polished and highly intelligent without flaunting it.

Totally out of character, I must admit I found myself more than a little intimidated by him for some reason or another. He engaged me in conversation on a screened-in back porch where we sipped homemade lemonade while watching the next-door neighbors frolicking at their water's edge.

Immediately I recognized the taller older gent and, yes, his white-haired mate. Water skiing seemed to be a popular family pastime.

There were others about, but I noticed those two right away. A pair of twelve-year-old-or-so-looking girls, one blonde and one brunette, slightly different heights, tossed around a giant beach ball.

Taken a back a bit, I did ask were the folks next door who I thought they appeared to be, and his reply was "Yes, those are our great next-door neighbors. They have lived there long before we had this place built . . . Such a lovely family, salt of the earth."

I sorta felt more out of place after verifying who the folks next door actually were. After lighting his aromatic Cuban cigar, he asked me what did I do for a living.

As he crossed his legs a certain way, for some unknown reason other than nerves, I parroted him and did likewise. I informed him

I had just gotten out of the Army and had recently started my new job at the investment firm.

Mind you, he was an important investment banker for a different, even larger firm. My ears later perked up whenever I'd hear his name mentioned on TV.

I shared I was awaiting my big check from Uncle Sam, although I was unsure exactly what I was going to do with it.

He puffed a couple of times and said in a matter-of-fact tone, "Perhaps you may want to look into purchasing a food cart." Manhattan city ordinances forbade big food trucks and trailers. "$10,000 should be a good down payment for you, but you'll need another $10,000 to successfully secure your business. I'd be more than willing to invest that amount if you like."

Don't ask me why, but here's my response: "A food cart? Why, I've never entertained such a thought in my life, but nevertheless, thank you for the suggestion. I'll think about it. On second thought, indubitably, I think I should turn your generous offer down."

Say what, you say? Yes, I made a complete fool of myself and regretted being such a idiot immediately after, and ever since.

My girl and her mom were standing in the doorway, and you should have seen them, rolling their eyes and giving me that dumb Homer Simpson look of "duh." I came across sounding like a bad imitation of TV's Amos & Andy's Kingfish!

My girl gave me holy hell when we got behind closed doors at home. Her mom did like the usual older island sistahs and stayed out of it.

Now fast forward twenty-two years. By then I was employed by a large and well-established garage door company in Houston. I got a call from dispatch, with a bizarre set of instructions. Why me? Don't know.

"You're going to be getting a call as soon as we hang up with instructions, just follow them to the letter. The fee, including your tip, has been prepaid in full."

"What's with all the I Spy?"

"Just do as directed, good-bye now."

Click.

"Ringggg".

I picked right up.

"Hello . . . Yes, this is he . . . Well, what is the address? Oh, there *is* no address? How am I supposed to find it then?"

"I am going to give you the address of the gas station nearest that location. When you arrive, call me back at this number . . . An agent will meet you there and then lead you to your destination."

"An agent, huh? Okay."

Like clockwork, someone slowly pulled up in front of me. He must have had my license number or been watching me all the time because he never got out of his vehicle.

He did make eye contact and motioned for me to follow him, which I did with a very queasy belly. There was a thirty-foot high wall covered by lots of ivy flanking that side of the interstate. It went on for a few miles. There was no way for anyone to tell what was on the other side of "the wall."

We drove down the opposite way of the wall and made a sharp right turn, followed by a quick left, ending at two huge black iron gates with no markings. The Secret Service agent must have put in a code; the gates parted like the Red Sea.

He hesitated until my truck was in and the gates slowly closed behind me. I tell you, it was something like finding Batman's secret cave.

We passed about half a mile. He then made a quick left and quicker right, and voila! We were in front of a long garage.

I got out with my tools and replaced a broken spring to the specific garage door as instructed. No one in the compound was seen. It was just me and the agent, who never got out of his car.

How ironic those two incidences were; although, they may have seemed, totally unrelated, they were so closely connected. I'm sure I guessed correctly, the identity of my seashore tall gentleman, but wasn't sure if he and his namesake lived together or not.

The first time, I was able to get a clear view of the recognizable tall, distinguished-looking gent, surrounded by loved ones in and at the water's edge. The second time there was no family member to be seen, but I had the once-in-a-lifetime opportunity to actually work on a job at one or both presidents' Texas compound.

If I played the numbers, I would have looked up "chance" and "odds", in the dream book and placed a boxed bet on each, but you know; I don't gamble.

CHAPTER 16

Cloverleaf Intersection

It was a beautiful sunny Sunday, Mother's Day. The San Antonio heat index topped at ninety-eight degrees.

A tiny Hispanic spot served great tacos which my mouth watered for. I ordered four tacos and, trying to eat more healthy, also added a chicken salad.

There was only one type of salad posted on the menu as simply SALAD, but when I saw the size of the salad container, my eyes got big. It was a family size for at least four grown men, filled with roasted white chicken chunks, plenty of iceberg lettuce, diced red tomatoes, cukes and a sprinkling of green onions and a healthy handful of shredded Mexican cheese, with loads of chopped eggs. I like thousand island dressing mixed with a little bit of blue cheese on the side, if they have it, and they did that Sunday. It was served with soda crackers. All that and the price was still low. Somebody had a heart for po' Hispanic folk.

As soon as I hit my truck, I gobbled up the four tacos, and couldn't eat another bite.

I thought, "I can't eat this salad now, and limp second-day lettuce is not worth saving. I'll need to find somebody to give this to."

A procession of vehicles slowly entered the cloverleaf intersection ramp. I could see ahead from midway in the line this thin White guy between twenty-eight and thirty-two years old seated on a tall overturned bucket, silently weeping his eyes out, as slowly passing cars and trucks drove right on by.

There was some sort of makeshift shanty behind him, back up under the corner of the overpass. I'd never seen anything like it before in my homeless hood haunts. Most likely, the police would not allow it in my neighborhood.

He had matted long brown hair but appeared to be wearing not so filthy-looking clothing, not that it mattered, just sayin'. The closer my truck inched towards him, I realized I couldn't just reach out and hand him anything.

It would be necessary for me to drive all the way around the back side, "get into some good trouble", double parking and calling him over closer to me. I hustled up to him from behind, with a neutral look on my face, kind eyes, and each corner of my mouth slightly upturned.

With all the traffic noise, I had to call out to him twice before reaching him. "Hey, hey there, I have some fresh chicken salad here for you, if you want it."

Without saying a word, he glanced up at me then leaped toward me with both hands held out. I handed it to him and also gave him a $5 bill, which the wind promptly blew away.

Beaming from ear to ear, he quickly chased it down. He wouldn't stop thanking me, to the point I began feeling a little embarrassed.

I told him, "Man, just enjoy it."

He extended his right hand for me to shake. Instead, I held up my hand in the 60s peace sign.

That wouldn't do, so I tried a fist bump and stuck out my elbow, mentioning the pandemic. Still no go.

He practically went into hysterics: "NO, man, I *gotta* shake your hand!"

Huh (sigh), he wore me down. I finally sheepishly extended my right hand, which he grabbed as firmly as possible without causing me permanent nerve damage, all the while thanking me without ceasing!

I told him I was just glad to be of some help and wished I could do more. I'm glad, early on, I was taught the value of food and to keep it for our own family.

If my folks wanted to give food away for any reason, then they had earned the right to do so, but not me. The way I saw them scuffling to keep things going, I think I may have considered food sacred or something.

When I'd be home alone, sometimes hungry kids used to come by our place, begging for food, if a bully, demanding it. Funny, that's one thing I refused to budge on.

You may be good at trash talkin', but I knew I had a ace in the hole every time, knowing I could truthfully say "At least I'm not always hungry, beggin' somebody for their food!"

I was pretty fast at running, seldom did I outrun the bigger boys, sometimes I got jacked up, but they all knew one thing for sure—nobody was getting my food! My mother made the best school outing lunches, and everybody knew it. I'd make sure to sit next to or across from the teacher or whichever mother chaperoned us kids.

The other kids mouths watered at the sight of my Oscar Myer boiled ham and Kraft American real cheese slice, sandwiched between white Wonder bread, spread thick with Miracle Whip, with Saran wrapped separately tomato and lettuce, some BBQ potato chips, a piece of fruit, usually a banana, my favorite, or a orange or. pear, never a apple, some Hostess Cupcakes or Twinkies and always a semi-frozen can of Faygo Red Pop, ummm ummm, ummm!

Thanks Ma.

Chapter 17

Grim Reaper

It had been a long, hectic day at work. I heated up a large Marie Callender's chicken pot pie, and washed it down with a big root beer vanilla ice cream float, took myself a long hot soak, and turned in early, which meant I slept loud and hard.

Maybe I should have listened to Mary J. instead of Easy E before drifting off to sleep, but it is what it is. I awoke in the middle of the night to a tapping at my outside French doors which opened onto a upstairs balcony.

Halloween was around the corner. The fall winds were howling while whipping it up outside.

I peeped open one eye to see what looked like a man dressed in a hooded coat with a stick in hand, tapping on my outer bedroom door. As the wind picked up, turning the taps into knocking, I sat straight up and said to myself, "This guy's got some damn nerve, he's really trying to come in on me!"

Fully awake and enraged, I reached under my pillow, grabbed my .45 ACP, removed the safety, and fired three quick shots.

Boom! Boom! Boom!

I then got up to see what was left of my brass-nerved potential home invader. Come to find out, "he" was a "it," a grim reaper, sickle-toting decoration from the next door neighbor's balcony, where they had stored their Halloween decorations for that next week.

Neighbors called the police, immediately summoning three Hispanic squad cars to my doors: one to the front door, one to the back, and one couple entered my home as I opened the front door.

"So tell us what happened."

"I woke up hearing a light tapping, which turned into heavy knocking on my upstairs bedroom French doors. The noise woke me up from a sound sleep, thinking I saw a man in a hood with a big stick outside of it, and as the wind picked up, the tapping turned into hard knocks, and so I felt threatened and defended myself! After firing three shots I opened up to find bits of the next door neighbor's Halloween grim reaper decoration. It had blown from their balcony over to mine. That's it."

In the sternest of tones, the shortest and most vocal of the uniformed officers said to me, "You know you're lucky don't you, that your room is upstairs because, if it was downstairs and you 'protected' yourself but shot somebody outside, we would have to take you in, regardless."

"Yeah. I know."

Thank goodness for my second-floor bedroom.

CHAPTER 18

"Dad Said"

Even today, whenever I find myself in a tight situation, especially out in these mean streets, I'm still haunted by what my dad said back when I was nine years old. I was given a brand new bike for my ninth birthday. It was slick, banana seat and all.

About a week after getting it, a older much bigger boy took it from me. In fact, he knocked me off it and told me, "This is my new bike now," and rode on off on it.

We lived in a condo complex named the Greens. I'd only seen that bully a few times but never confrontationally.

I cried big croc tears, feeling more humiliated than anything. It happened to be a Saturday, so lucky for me, my dad was home. Now if only my ma had been home, she would have handled it way differently, politically correctly, embarrassing me more than I already was.

Back in the day, my dad used to be quite the bully himself growing up. At least that was the reputation he had according to one of my cousins who knew him back when. He showed me no mercy but instead, asked me whose bike it was.

I shyly said, "Mine."

He said to "Go get it then!"

I sniffled and snotted, before finally drying up, and began whining about how much bigger and older he was than me, maybe around eleven or so.

My dad's further instructions to me were "I don't care how old he is or how big he is. I did not scuffle to buy you that new bike for your birthday to just let some punk take it from you! Now you dry up, and march back out there, and demand he give it back to you. You're the rightful owner, not him!"

He added, "Nobody's going to fight your battles for you. No! Every man has gotta do his own fighting! He may end up needing help, but he's gotta at least try on his own first."

Mind you, this was before everybody started packin' to settle petty scores.

Still, I was afraid but knew, by how serious my dad spoke, I had no choice but to face my Goliath. I'd rather face any bully than my dad.

I wiped my face, blew my nose, and stood up straight then went out to demand my property back. Little did I know my dad tailed me.

I wished I couldn't find the guy, but there he was, riding around the Greens, yukking it up with some other big boys on bikes, having a good ole time on my new bike.

I shouted out to him, "I came for my bike!"

I had my little fists balled up at my sides.

He stopped and stared at me, saying, "Oh yeah, come an' get it!"

I was trembling inside but walked my bravest on over there. He dared me to say it again.

I did, and he snatched me right up.

Right then, my pop popped out from behind a corner building and told the thief to let go of "his son," say "sorry," swear never to bother me again, let alone ever dare touch my new bike again!

Maaannn, I felt ten feet tall! I learned a lifelong lesson to boot. Always, "Do the right thing." (Thanks, Spike.)

Others may think so, but that day I *knew* I had the best dad in the whole wide world!

Thanks Dad.

CHAPTER 19

Sole Brotha

By now you know my feelings on giving grown men money or buying them anything with my money. Well I must admit, there was one exception to my steadfast rule, just between you and me.

On a off day, I craved some good ole juicy KFC. I went to one a little further out, closer to White folk's territory because it was true, the meat tasted fresher.

I was able to park in front. As I walked in, I caught a glimpse of a short, small boned Hispanic looking male. It was hard to tell his age, but I'd guess maybe 19 or 20, barely grown, but grown enough. He was no doubt an illegal, the way he lurked about barely out of sight, but so starved, he hoovered around, looking ashamed, while silently begging for food all at the same time.

I ordered my usual, dark meat special this time with fries, I figured the high sodium and fat was about equal in the mashed potatoes with gravy as in the fries, so I may as well have what I had a taste for. I ordered a large Sprite and a cup a iced water to wash things down with. Of course, I got it to go, preferring to eat alone, in the privacy of my own cooled off van, rather than sit inside with gawkers, or worse homeless beggars, which always spoiled the mood.

While exiting, I went straight to my van and sat under the ac, where I got a clearer view of the waif. He was a Hispanic male in tattered clothes, with long, stringy black hair, and smudged up sad face. He didn't look Mexican to me, maybe from El Salvador, or Ecuador, or one of those doors, located further south of Mexico.

I tried my best to avoid looking him in the face, but the mere fact of knowing he was there kept drawing me in. Why not just drive away? I wanted to eat my piping hot food, that's why! I started to just call him over and give him my food, but it was exactly what I wanted, so I hopped out the van and ran in and ordered him a 2 piece leg dinner with mashed potatoes and gravy and Cole slaw, extra biscuit with honey and a big iced water, as not to dehydrate my lil' amigo.

I know I'd think nothing of tossing scraps to a hungry dog; why wouldn't I feed a fellow human being, whether legal or illegal?

By now my special treat was stone cold, but I choked it on down while watching him stuffing his face. When I lifted my cup as if to toast, he smiled back a Jack o lantern grin and did likewise; making it all worth my while.

Chapter 20

I Believe in Miracles

My previous boss seemed determined to add extra hoops for me to jump through as that company continued expanding. There were a few things I simply refused to do over any extended period and others I'd never do.

He'd convinced me to relocate from my beloved Houston in order to accept a considerable raise in pay and an impressive-sounding title, although I would prefer for you to "Show me the money!" over a title any day. Once settled in my new position, certain secrets were revealed to me after the fact, sort of like false advertisement.

After moving, I was between a rock and a hard place but tried to hold on to prevent having to pack up and begin all over again. My good ole boy boss set up a meeting with me at a steak house. He helped run someone else's conglomerate business with a chain across America.

I always dreaded his random visits. I hated his revenue reviews.

I could never satisfy him with my sell numbers, even though I was selling more expensive product than his average other workers. While driving to my destination, something kept urging me to "pull over."

I can't explain it, but I call it my "queasy belly." My mother calls it the Holy Spirit. You might call it intuition, do men have that? I thought that was a female thing like cramps.

Suddenly I obeyed and cut into a vacant spot in front of a gas station. Around ten garage door company names filled the screen.

As I worked my way down the list, most were closing, some said submit a resume, there were a few no answers, but that final call was answered by the owner of this particular company. Unbelievable!

I stated "job hunting" as the purpose of my call. It's true, how desperate times calls for desperate measures.

The guy on the other end said, "Funny you should call now. I am usually not in the office answering calls this time of day." He went on to say, "My most experienced installer had a stroke, and it doesn't look like he's coming back anytime soon, if at all."

He said he needed an experienced installer; and if I was one, was I currently employed? I said yes, but I expected to be unemployed within the week, if the meeting I was now headed for ended the way I expected. To help sweeten the pot, I rattled off my twenty years of experience.

My total recall enables me to remember back when I was only 2.5 years old, and an old uncle granted my request and sneaked me some of his while watching the channel 7 nightly news, daily-sipped Johnny Walker Red, causing me to bump into walls like a pinball, which tickled the hell outta ole unk. My parents were saving toward their first home, and we temporarily lived with him and his wife, on my dad's side, at the time. My mother, not at all amused, stepped up and instructed him to never give me another drop of any type of alcohol, ever again! He gave his word he wouldn't and kept it.

I'm glad I'm generally not one to judge, I believe in "live and let live" and "to each his own," and so the same should apply to me.

I shouldn't have to apologize, or feel obligated to always explain, I just happen to be a guy who doesn't indulge, that's it. I can't tell you how many times, especially in the military I've heard other men say to my face, "I don't trust a man who don't drink." Ignorant as hell!

That initial feeling of loss of control must have really struck and stuck with me all these years because I did not experiment with any drug, drink, or smoke for the rest of my life, including those teen years.

I told my soon-to-be new boss, "I don't smoke, dip or chaw anything, drink booze, or take non-prescribed drugs."

I shared a few more important details related to why I was displeased with the recent way things had taken a turn for the worse with my current employer. Come to find out, he shared that he too had worked for the same company before starting up his own business. He left for the same reason: pressure to sell more.

Small world. Then I threw in a bombshell.

If he wanted to check on my honesty, he could pull up a YouTube video where my company name was mentioned in a AZ garage door honesty sting operation. His silence let me know he was interested in what I had to say.

At the end of the conversation, I told him I'd probably work until the end of the week to make sure I'd get my last check.

He said, "All our employees must wear our company logo tee shirts. What size do you wear? It sounds like you may be able to start on Monday. Am I right?"

Shocked, I could hardly believe my ears. Was he really hiring me over the phone, sight unseen, without a resume or letterhead recommendation?

A-M-A-Z-I-N-G!

"I'm not trying to look a gift horse in the mouth, but let me be sure I understand. Are you hiring me over the phone?"

He then said, "You betcha! My back's up against the wall here, and honestly, I like what you're saying so far. I trust my gut instinct."

I couldn't help but think of my own gut reactions.

"I'm saying *yes* and welcome aboard. You'll call me over this weekend to finalize things before Monday, right?"

"Yes, sir, and thanks!"

Man! I felt on top of the world! No one could have told me that conversation would have ended with me being a new hire over the phone, especially me being a Black guy hired by a White owner of the company, no less.

I like to think my many good deeds contributed to my newfound good fortune, but some may argue there are no coincidences. My new boss even had a contract with a national chain of preset priced doors at area warehouses.

So no more "sell, sell, sell!" I would no longer have to deal with beating little old blue-haired ladies over the head with higher-priced items they didn't need.

In fact, several of them have told me flat out they like my soft-sell method. In any event, I am very grateful for the miracles that have brought me to this point in my life.